MW01227997

TURTLE DOVE DONE DROOPED HIS WINGS

A GULLAH TALE OF FIGHT OR FLIGHT - BOOK 2
GEECHEE LITERATURE SERIES

RON DAISE

RON AND NATALIE DAISE

CONTENTS

Ron and Natalie Daise
Geechee Literature Series
209 Whitehall Avenue
Georgetown, SC 29440

© 2020 Ron Daise

Cover design: Barbara Smullen
Text design: Barbara Smullen
Typography: Barbara Smullen

First printing, May 2022
ISBN: 9798819241783
Independently published

Published in the United States

Ron Daise

ACKNOWLEDGMENTS

"Turtle Dove Done Drooped His Wings" is dedicated to Elaine Nichols for recommending me and Bob Jewell for allowing me the opportunity to engage in a fantastic voyage!

I extend immense gratitude to my wife and children, Natalie, Sara, and Simeon Daise. Also, to Paul Garbarini, Johnny A. Ford, Michele Moore, Joyce Cirino, Stephanie Atkinson, Viki Richardson, Linda Ketron, and Karen Chandler for reading, commenting, and encouraging.

FOREWORD

Turtle Dove Done Drooped His Wings, A Gullah Tale of Fight or Flight by Ron Daise is a lyrical ode to our Gullah Geechee oral tradition, told with the vividness of Aesop's fables and intimacy of an old family story passed down like a precious heirloom. The keen character development and Gullah language dialogue brought to mind personal friends and relatives in place of the characters. Readers familiar with Lowcountry living will catch the colloquialisms and be delighted to hear many phrases that we're accustomed to hearing only in conversations amongst ourselves. Yet, one does not have to be a Lowcountry native or speaker of our colorful dialects to immerse oneself into this moral tale. While spoken from the mouths of birds, this story gives voice to innate human dilemmas.

As a Gullah language instructor at Harvard University, I'm often asked for recommendations of Gullah literary works that I enjoy and consider authentic representations of our people, language, and culture. Not only do I recommend Ron Daise's *Turtle Dove Done Drooped His Wings*, I will see to it that my own students experience for themselves why I regard Ron Daise as a Gullah griot of the highest order. The impressiveness of this book is rivaled only by its author.

Sunn m'Cheaux
    Charleston, South Carolina
    April 2022

INSPIRATION

The roosting places which the Carolina Turtles prefer are among the long grasses found growing in abandoned fields, at the foot of dry stalks of maize, or on the edges of meadows, although they occasionally resort to the dead foliage of trees, as well as that of different species of evergreens. But in all these places they rise and fly at the approach of man, however dark the night may be, which proves that the power of sight which they then possess is very great.

John James Audubon

Even the stork in the sky knows her appointed seasons, and the dove, the swift and the thrush observe the time of their migration. But my people do not know the requirements of the Lord.

Jeremiah 8:7

CHAPTER ONE

THE NEWNESS OF THE DAY BEGAN TO PEEK OUT FROM BEHIND THE shadows. The wildlife sniffed a difference in the air, the breezes, the sunlight. Moment by moment, they sensed the scenery of the Lowcountry marsh grass, water ways, and horizon transform to the splendid beauty of the colors of the male Painted Bunting. Turtle Dove paced and "turr-turred" around and around the base of Angel Oak, the sacred meeting grounds. Bowing his head, then looking up and moving on to another space, he cooed affirmations that all would be well. That those who gathered would fully know their appointed season. That he would be able at all times to speak calmly during strife or noise and to bring about healing and peace.

Barred Owl, knowing that great Action brings about great Change, had been awaiting the moment. She'd heard that a new law of the land had been issued. A regional Audubon Rookery had been established, unlike any other rookery anywhere else. And a Great Council had been assembled to determine the best way to govern and watch over it.

Birds and reptiles, insects and fishes all received the news with amazement. Barred Owl rejoiced with a hoot. Other animals sang and howled songs of happiness, while others shrieked and hissed with annoyance that their group had not been so favored. Some even hmf- ed with indifference. But Barred Owl just watched and waited.

When the Great Council met for the very first time, feathers plumed, wings unfurled, and chests uplifted. Bystanders watched admiringly, observing the expressions of pride and determination on the Council members' faces. Barred Owl, however, peered below the feathers. What she saw made her blink unexpectedly. "Oh, my," she thought to herself. "Every bird loves to hear himself sing. But the best sounding choir only needs one soloist. Wherever there's discord, there's distrust and disunity. Hoot-hoo. Hoot-hoo."

The skies above sparkled as blue as the oceans of distant lands as the council members arrived. Below the Angel Oak branches, however, the atmosphere at times became dark and dreary like the skies above slave ships that sailed through howling storms.

"No, we should not call ourselves 'Audubon Rookery,'" Hooded Merganser snapped angrily. "Before we start doing anything, we must find a name that better says who we are."

"What? Another name?" Bald Eagle replied. "We are birds! What better name defines us?"

"Oh, please pardon me, Wonderful Winged One," Hooded Merganser continued in a recklessly pompous tone. "I don't mean to offend you. But, you see, the word 'Audubon' communicates being French American. Are any of you here French American?" He looked to those gathered for a response, and the council members shook their heads.

Bald Eagle asked, "So-o-o-o-o?"

"Well, using the full name, 'John James Audubon Rookery' fits us better, you know, like birds that flock together. John James Audubon was a French American. He was born in Dominique, the country that's known today as Haiti. His paintings and writings about American birds are the legacy that our name honors. But it's his Haitian heritage that is more closely connected to the heritage of Birds of the Lowcountry, whom, thanks to you, we are honored to represent."

"You are welcome. And thank you," Bald Eagle responded with compassion. "But this Rookery, as you stated, is indeed named in honor of John James Audubon. Those who do not know this hopefully will come to know it as the Great Council begins to do what it has been brought together to do."

Anhinga interrupted. "Perhaps we should talk about this matter after the reporters leave, Hooded Merganser," she whispered. "Don't you think that would be the Better Bird thing to do?"

"The name 'Audubon Rookery' has become the name of the law," Bald Eagle continued. "Let's not slow this flight down before it takes off..."

"But our ancestors came from West Africa," Hooded Merganser argued, "not from Fr..."

"No more 'buts' about this matter, please. In fact, if any one of you wants to slow down the progress that has been made over the past two years. The progress that has brought us to this great moment today, please, please, fly away now. You are free to search for other paths that would lead to where you may think we need to travel."

Silence swept across the gathering. Rookery members and bystanders had begun to stare irritatingly as the discussion continued.

"Are we ready to move forward and tell the world who we are?"

"Why, yes," Hooded Merganser said quietly, with eyes looking only in front of him. "As you wish, Bald Eagle. As you wish."

Wood Stork, standing nearby, called out, "Hey, we got this, Hooded Merganser! You know, when Bald Eagle talked about this idea years ago, everything that you said was brought to his attention over time. The shorter name is just easier to remember."

He looked reassuringly at the silent Hooded Merganser and then continued. "If we all work together, and not get Bald Eagle upset, we can make sure that everyone knows about the connection of Lowcountry birds with Haitian birds whenever the name Audubon Rookery is mentioned. Sound good to you?"

Hooded Merganser never said a mumblin word. Thoughts of annoyance had come a-knockin in his heart and mind!

Momentarily, as other topics were discussed, Hooded Merganser turned his head to the right, reached back with his beak to his tail, and plucked out a feather. Turning back around, he released the feather from his mouth and watched it fall slowly to the ground in front of him. A look of dissatisfaction -- an *I-don't-know-why-I'm-being-made-to-*

feel-embarrassed-about   speaking-my-mind-but-someone-is-going-to-pay-for-this! look of dissatisfaction -- painted his face. His body stiffened and stayed that way throughout the meeting. It relaxed only somewhat to nod goodbye and smile as everyone departed.

Turtle Dove's throat muscles tightened as he'd watched Hooded Merganser's silent but defiant declaration. He could not coo. He could not turr-turr as his mind replayed the tensions of the day's interac- tions. "Tomorrow," he reasoned to himself, "I'll get them to see what's being said and to hear what's being done."

And there was evening, and there was morning—the first day.

CHAPTER TWO

AT THE NEXT MEETING, GREAT COUNCIL MEMBERS NOMINATED GREAT Blue Heron, Hooded Merganser, Starling, and Anhinga to lead the flock. A vote would follow.

"I'll support you," Wood Stork confided to Hooded Merganser. "Just tell the others the ways that you think can make this rookery the best place for our hatchlings to thrive."

"I'm going to pray that the Elder SkyHawks keep us grounded," Hooded Merganser proclaimed. "This new rookery will give every Lowcountry bird the recognition we so rightly deserve. With me, we'll seize the moment, doing what we need to do and in the ways we need to do it."

Turtle Dove stepped toward Hooded Merganser. "That's a great plan," he said. "Now, are you saying that our elders will guide us with their first getting input from the younger hatchlings? Or do you think youths should just trust the leadership of the aged Birds on the Wing -- without question?"

Slightly startled by the question, Merganser tried to respond, but Starling -- sometimes regaled as Starling of Bird Land -- began crowing. "Make no mistake," Starling said. "Because of the flight commands I've given to the Birds of Prey Patrol, the Wade in the Water

Webbers, and the Birds-of-paradise Playas, these Bird Land organizations -- that I started, now -- are becoming the best known throughout Birdom. Follow my lead, yes, follow my lead, and all who know me will know about the Audubon Rookery and what WE can do. What WE can do for every bird who has gone on to the Nest Not Built by Beaks and for those who are still flapping our wings."

Anhinga stepped forward. Power-stancing, she spread her wings as though she were sunning herself. Closing them slowly, she paused and then spoke. "No, colleagues, this just is not the right time for me. Great Blue Heron has led the wider world in knowing the importance of us Rulers of the Air in these parts for years," Anhinga said. "I thank the one who nominated me, but in this company and at this time, I elect to withdraw." Squawking and the rustling of feathers sounded in the breeze. Then Anhinga continued, "I cast my support for Great Blue Heron."

Surprised, Great Blue Heron looked at Anhinga and lowered her head questioningly. Anhinga's matter-of-fact smile prompted Great Blue Heron to turn toward the Great Council.

"Well, those who know me, know that I am who you see," she said. "For those who are unfamiliar with me, please know this -- I will do my best to serve as your leader if I'm elected, as I've done in all my previous leadership positions. And if I'm not your choice, I will work untiringly to support whoever is."

The moment had arrived. Many of the birds patted their feet and moved their heads from side to side. They voted by trilling, cawing, and whistling as each candidate's name was called. The loudest response would declare the winner.

Following Great Blue Heron's overwhelming election, she opened the envelope Bald Eagle had left with Wood Stork, a member of the National Order of Fowl History, to give to the new leader. It identified the Mission of the Great Council.

"Well, well, well," Great Blue Heron sighed after reading it. She then read aloud: "Birds of the Lowcountry, we are about to begin a great journey. It may be the flight of our lives. The new law is designed to help us to glide, flap, and soar at altitudes some of us have only dreamed of reaching. All eyes will be on us, now! When we meet again, we must begin to determine our Thrust, that is, the action that will make us move through the air and continue flying!"

"Put on your wings," Anhinga said confidently and then began whistling, "When we get to heaven…"

Others joined her in the response, "… gonna put on our wings…"

"That's right," Great Blue Heron said, "We've got to put on our wings. Fa true!"

Cedar Waxwing called out in a low rasp that could only be heard by those nearby. "Hey, Mergansa, don't even think about changing our name, please. We don't need *drag;* we need *lift*! Yes, suh, please don't pull us down like you did yesterday. Titter, titter, titter. Chuckle, chuckle, chuckle."

Hurt and embarrassed, Merganser lashed back. "Oh, so you making jokes, huh? What's your song, Cedar Waxwing? Huh? You gotta song? A bird doesn't sing because it has an answer. It sings because it has a song. And you know what? You don't got no beenyah song, do you? Besides, you won't be here year-round anyway to get this Rookery launched. You just a comeyah. So fly away. Take your jokes with ya, Comeyah. Fly away."

Watching and listening from a distance, Barred Owl thought of something she'd heard her grandfather say, "'The arrow strikes one bird down, but the flock remains.'" She reasoned, "Walk together, birdies, don't you get weary. Please walk together."

And there was evening, and there was morning—the second day.

CHAPTER THREE

THE GROUNDS BELOW THE FAR-REACHING ANGEL OAK LIMBS WERE charged with energy, excitement, and ego -- oh my! Great Council members arrived ready to work. And Great Blue Heron began the session with an important and unexpected announcement.

"Bald Eagle has informed me that all ideas will need to be presented over the next four days, and a selection will be made on the following day. Also, the Council member whose efforts help most to determine our Thrust will receive the first Broad-winged Hawk Distin- guished Service Award."

A chorus of woops, jeeps, and whip-poor-wills followed. "Now who wants to pitch your idea first? I know it's been top on your minds since yesterday." Looking around after a brief moment of silence, Great Blue Heron asked, "Starling, how about you?"

"No, not yet," Starling answered. "I'll wait." If he listened to the others first, he thought, his presentation, by far, would be the most sensational and dynamic.

Tufted Titmouse raised her right wing and waited for Blue Heron's nod to speak.

"When I would fly over the Bill Saunders House of Hope in Johns Island, all the birds who roosted in the trees nearby would tell me things," she said. "They'd say they tried to eat healthy. But if they ate only what the People threw on the grounds near the trash cans, they would get sick, and some would die.

"They said the crumbs they'd pull out of the bags and boxes from fast-food restaurants and neighborhood stores were salty and fried and sweet. So, they'd fly back up into the trees and leave that People food alone!"

"I know that's right," Red-winged blackbird said. "If it ain good fa ya, hunnah betta leave em lone!"

"That's what I'm talking about," Tufted Titmouse continued. "Some foods just fill us with preservatives that'll take us to our graves sooner than necessary. They'll make you moan the song, 'Maybe the last time. I don't know...' Natural foods, now, make us thrive and keep us alive.

"Don't preserve me, please! No. No. No. No. No. Our Thrust should be programs about eating right, feeling right, being right."

Waving both of her uplifted wings and her head back-and-forth to the left and then to the right and speaking in a singsong manner, she said, "Only healthy birds can take to the air and flap our wings like we just don't care."

Council members laughed and shook their heads. "Okay, okay, who agrees with Tufted Titmouse?" Great Blue Heron asked. "And what can be added to this idea to make it tasty like a good Frogmore Stew?"

Tufted Titmouse looked and waited, fearing that no one else had been interested. A burst of red flew quickly down to the meeting space from a top branch. "Call on Bobolink," Cardinal said. "I think Bobolink would have a lot to say on this matter."

When Bobolink heard her name mentioned, she blinked her eyes and said, "Food is so important. Yes, it is. Yes, it is! Now, I know I'm a comeyah. But you need to listen to what I have to say about why I *come yah* year after year. To feast on those grains of rice. The delicious and delectable grains of Carolina Gold in the rice fields of Georgetown, SC. And the scrumptious and savory rice grains in the fields of Riceboro, GA. Ooo-wee, they would make you smack your Mama! And they were good for you and good to your taste buds, too. Once we had filled ourselves with food that stuck to our tiny ribs and filled our minds with strength from listening to the songs of the enslaved

Africans who worked in those fields, we could feel the V-formation coming on. And we were ready to lift our wings and journey on. To see what the end was gonna be!"

Tufted Titmouse, pleased to hear Bobolink's story, pursed her beaks together and shook her head up and down. She thought about how Mama birds knew what plants to search for to calm their babies' colicky bellies. And how to gather Spanish moss to wrap around their mates' feet when they had been chased by some pesky cat. Yes, yes, Mama birds of the Lowcountry knew exactly what to do to bring the pressure down.

Red-cockaded woodpecker's sudden and rapid tap-tap-tapping in a nearby pine tree, however, just about raised Tufted Titmouse's blood pressure to a dangerous level. He calmed down when the ruckus stopped. Aware that he had gotten everyone's attention, Red-cockaded woodpecker tapped again with fanfare.

"Tap! Tap, Tap, Tap, Tap! Tap, Tap!" He quickly flew to join others below Angel Oak. These trees. The architecture of Lowcountry trees is something we should really pay attention to," he mused. "They're unlike trees anywhere else. There's Loblolly pine. Birch. Water oak. Live oak. There's Magnolia. Bald Cypress, Fig, Pecan, and so many more.

"They are beautiful! They are homes for our families. When enemies come after us, they're our hiding place. We find food in them and around their trunks. And from our perch on their limbs, we can hear People stories about the world, about places we've never visited. From treetops, many of us learn to fly. Trees could be our Thrust -- someway, somehow."

Moved by the soliloquy, Crow began to caw. "You know...I thought it was going to be my last day on Earth!" Crow muttered slowly, as if fearful to recall a dreadful memory. "My two siblings and I had waited patiently in our nest. Mama and Daddy had been gone a long time. They both went looking for food, they'd said. Mildred somehow stepped out first, while we were sleeping. She was Daddy's favorite. 'Come on out,' she called back. 'Wake up, yall!' When we woke and heard her, Henry started climbing the nest wall, then fell back down to the bottom. He rolled over then slowly stood back up.

"'Yall so slow,'" Mildred chided. 'Get a move on! It looks so good out here. You gotta see it!'

"Henry started jumping again and again and flapping faster and faster until before he knew it, he found himself up on the top of the nest wall. He teetered back and forth, getting his balance. And then he jumped onto the limb, joining Mildred.

"Mama showed up first with some grubs. She gave one to each of them, told them how proud she was to see them there, and asked them to wait while she checked on me. I was chirping like a scared maniac. Mildred saw Daddy approaching, I'm told, and then leaped into the air. Of course, she started flying as though she had been doing so for years. Daddy didn't even have to help her. Mama flew down to be with her when she'd landed safely on the ground.

"'That's my girl!' Daddy called down from the limb. 'Where's your brother?' he asked Henry. 'Scaredy Bird still in the nest,' Henry chuckled. 'Not for long,' Daddy shot back. He leaned over the edge, grabbed me by the scruff and set me next to my brother. 'Boys, this is an experience you'll remember for the rest of your life. It's the day to learn to do what birds were born to do!'

"'I'm ready,' Henry yelled. And right before my eyes, he jumped! He started falling, falling, falling. Then he moved his wings like we'd seen Mommy and Daddy doing when they left or returned home. In a short while, he got in the groove and was on his own.

"When I looked down and saw Mildred and Mom, I felt woozie and started slowly tip, tip, tipping back toward the nest. 'No-o-o-o-! Not me, not now,' I cried, but Dad was hearing none of it. None of it! He nudged me with his beak. And, like my sister and brother, soon, I, too, was having that experience that I cannot forget. Oh, I'll remember it for the rest of my life. Not because I was courageous or determined about it. Hmpf, I thought I was going to die! And my brother still laughs about that moment to this day. But that doesn't matter. What matters is that I did it. It's a moment I'm sure all of us can relate to. And like we heard from Reddy Woodpecker, most of us did it from the top of a tree!"

Turtle Dove bobbed his head up and down, up and down, then spoke. "Food *and* trees. Food *in* trees." He smiled and opened his wings upward in a gesture of amazement. "Trees *housing* birds. Birds *housing* the strengths that sustain families. These are linkages. These are connections."

"No, I beg to disagree," Starling stated snarkily. "The time before us cannot be spent reflecting on things that have already been done. These are not times to continue doing the same things over and over again. That is not Thrust. That is Reinvention. The Bird Land Birds of Prey Patrol have documented every treetop in this region. The Wade in the Water Webbers have written recipe books about the natural food supplies in the wetlands, the waterways, the watersheds. And…"

"But perhaps," Turtle Dove began softly, "other groups may have done similar things…"

"These *other* groups are marsh grass organizations, mind you, working throughout each community from the roots up. They have devoted endless hours to…"

"…but. perhaps…," Turtle Dove intoned, after turning his head slowly to lock eyes with his interrupter and to smile ever pleasantly. The brusque disruption had torpedoed the concentration of his delivery. To refocus, Turtle Dove continued to complete his thought with speech that became clipped, diction that pulsated, and a voice that, at times, crescendoed. "…Perhaps," he began again, "they. have done. similar things. but. Have.Not.captured.Every Nuance.or.EVERY Activity. Could THAT be possible?"

Pleased that he had been able to successfully relay the words that had been revolving in his head in search of an exit and that he'd done so in a way that all should be able to comprehend, Turtle Dove relaxed. He inhaled deeply and released cleansing breaths.

Others thought he'd been agitated. Some had been taken aback. He, to the contrary, eagerly awaited the return to conversation, perhaps even to new conversations where, as he'd known since childhood, he'd hear what others saw and see what others heard.

New Great Council conversations would occur another time, however. Great Blue Heron called for the meeting to adjourn.

And there was evening, and there was morning—the third day.

CHAPTER FOUR

next day.

"Quack, quack, quack," Ruddy duck announced her entrance to the gathering of Tufted Titmouse and Hooded Merganser. "Quack, quack, quack. Now, what dirt are you two dishing this morning? I know you are."

"No, we're just wondering what got into Turtle Dove yesterday," Tufted Titmouse stated. "Did he drink some cordgrass cocktail? He seemed mighty upset. I mean big-time upset, cut-throat upset!!"

"Really?" Ruddy Duck responded. "No, I think he was just explaining himself. He gets that way sometimes when he's getting his thoughts out. Now, when he gets mad, he'll cut you with his words, and you won't know you're bleeding until you look down and see red rivulets all around you. What he said yesterday was just at a slower pace than usual. Did anyone get upset about it? That wasn't anything to trouble your mind about."

"What upsets me is seeing him raise that right wing," said Hooded Merganser.

They watched as Anhinga sauntered toward them, and they opened their group, so she'd feel welcomed.

"What bothers you about the right wing?" Tufted Titmouse asked. "What's got you so paranoid?"

"When the wing goes up, I know he's about to come down, and I mean DOWN, on something someone said or did!"

"No, no, no, no," Tufted Titmouse countered. "That's not it. I find that his questions help us to see things that the speaker may have meant to say -- but didn't. Or sometimes his questions point out that maybe two or more of us had been saying the same thing, but we'd thought we were saying different things because we'd been using different words or expressions. Like the time when he came across my husband and me fussing on the clothesline.

"I'd said, 'Hey, Boo, you wanna fly north and dine on the red Sour Sally perennials in the fields near Navassa?' He played the doofus, but I knew he knew what I was talking about. So, I explained, like I seem to have to do everytime we talk about it, that Sour Sally was the Red sorrel that the People children would eat. They would throw a bunch of green stems in their mouths, chew them a few seconds, then spit them out. Why they did that, I don't know! I'm glad they'd leave those de-e-e-licious red berries and fruit for me to nyam on, though.

"Then, to make the idea even more inviting, I told him, "And we can spend some time with the Fulvous Family and catch up on all the new whistles they learned during their last migration.'

"And he said, 'Nah, Honey, I've been thinking about us traveling to our honeymoon tree near the Cape Fear River. We can nibble on some juicy snails. You can grab one end, I'll grab the other, and we can reunite with smooches when we meet in the middle.' "Then he hunched his shoulders over and over again and blinked at me like that was going to change my mind. Oh, no, it did not!

"Besides, sometimes he thinks he knows more about the Birds of the Lowcountry community where I'm from than we Birds of the Lowcountry community where I from do. I eat slugs *cause* he loves slugs. Lowland birds love us up some Sour Sally flowers and fruit, now! That's the food that makes our bellies want to dance. Slugs? Mm-mmm!

"Well, anyway, Turtle Dove listened to us go at it for a while, with neither one of us backing down about what we wanted the other one to do. Then Turtle Dove turned to us and said, 'Would you mind if I asked a question, please?' We'd forgotten he was even there. First, we looked at each other, then we both nodded at him.

"'Why don't you consider flying to the Cape Fear River and spending a night of wedded bliss, then continue the vacay with a Sour Sally brunch on your return flight tomorrow? The two locations are just a few breast strokes away from each other.'

"What he'd suggested made so much sense! And my hubby and me had been so convinced that the things we'd said weren't even closely related. Now, the beauty of his suggestion is that I got to bring back some seeds and slugs for the Goldfinch family whose forest habitat had been devastated during a controlled burn. But that's not the point. What was it that Turtle Dove had done first?"

"He'd asked a question. Right? Now, isn't that just what I said?" Ruddy Duck quacked. "Just remember -- don't trip him up when he has a thought to express. That could lead to a scene like we witnessed yesterday."

Anhinga's eyes widened, and her head twitched in recognition of a revelation. She nodded, dapped wings with the others, then meandered toward another crowd and launched an unusual discussion.

"Well, hello, my fellow Telephone Line Onlookers," she said. "This is something I think we should consider. We may be called upon to promote businesses, sometimes non-Lowcountry Bird businesses, that produce products that are for Lowcountry birds."

"Uhn, uhn, uhn," Seagull squawked. "Businesses by Lowcountry birds and for Lowcountry birds is what we should be about. "You don't even have to have a big and beautiful Lowcountry bird brain like mine to think that!"

Anhinga continued, "But if merchandise is made that promotes us, then others will want it and then would want to be like us."

"We don't want everybody else to be like us," Seagull bucked. "If that happens, we might forget who we are. And if we forget who we are, others will start telling us who we are. And then...and then...well, other birds and other animals will become the Audubon Rookery. Even if there's nothing authentically Lowcountry bird about them. Who else sees things this way?"

Before others could respond, Great Blue Heron called for the Great Council members to gather. Wood Stork stepped forward to pitch his proposal.

"It is critical for us to realize that the known ways for animal-kind to observe us at the new heights we'll be flying are outside of the familiar," he explained. "I think we should encourage only Lowcountry birds to receive Air Patrol training in the new category for the altitude that we alone will ascend to flying."

"That's right," Great Blue Heron countered. "We ourselves may need to undergo some flight training." Her eyes opened wider as she looked out to the differing age groups of Great Council members. "Others will be visiting our Audubon Rookery in our natural habitats, but if they want to see us as we fly at our new level, or if we ourselves want to get there to enjoy the New Altitude, we'll have to learn some new tricks."

The sight of Turtle Dove winging in late caught everyone's attention. He'd had no idea that his tardiness would derail discussion or that it would be destructively utilized to set him up as a lame duck.

"I'm so sorry, so sorry!" Turtle Dove sighed. "I was...

Purposefully changing topics, as he reflected on his pre-meeting conversation, Hooded Merganser asked, "Had a hard time unwinding yesterday, Turtle Dove? Got to sleep kind of late? You're usually the first one here."

"Oh, thank you," Turtle Dove began. The answers to your questions are 'no' and 'no,' but...."

"We were having a great discussion. Thought you'd be raising your wing about now, anyway...," Hooded Merganser said before turning quickly to Wood Stork. "Wood Stork, what were you saying?" In a heartbeat, Hooded Merganser pivoted back to Turtle Dove. "Pardon me, Turtle Dove, you were saying, 'but....'"

Feeling flustered by not being able to sense any meaning to the volley of conversation that Hooded Merganser was leading, Turtle Dove looked around the table and began tasting the air. He'd meant to inform the others about the People talk he'd heard as he ate a breakfast of sunflowers in a neighborhood bird feeder. The People had said that a friend's company, Bobolink Bird Feed, was going to start mixing plastic in their ingredients to cut down on costs. They'd said their friend had offered some kind of kickback to someone on the Audubon Rookery's Great Council if the Council member would smooth the way for their business to culturally appropriate the market.

"Could we get back on-topic, please?" Wood Stork asked, looking to Great Blue Heron for affirmation. "This will involve new flight patterns," he continued. "Officers may need to enforce speed violations on the crosswinds. Or upwind travel in air currents filled with migratory flocks. But one of the main challenges is the development of new Aerial Markers. When placed appropriately at numerous altitudes, these will serve as enticements for others to visit, to learn about our lifestyles, our history, our heritage."

Starling raised his wing. When Great Blue Heron looked his way, he said, "And the Birds-of-paradise Playas will know exactly how to get this organized. In all of my Bird Land affiliations, members are well trained and ready, and the Playas are experts in computer graphics and design technology."

The braggadociousness prompted Commissioners to glance toward each other disapprovingly.

To alter the ambience, Seagull squawked with admiration, "He's the star in the East on Christmas morn!"

Starling stoically deflected his compliment by nodding with reservation then looking away. Inwardly, however, he readied to receive an expected groundswell of praise.

"But I'd think whoever is used would need overall guidance from the Air Patrol, isn't that right, Wood Stork?" Turtle Dove asked.

First, shooting a scowl at Turtle Dove and then a look of poise and professionalism at Great Blue Heron, a perturbed Starling said, "Why, of course, we would operate under the guidelines of any overseeing agency. However, I'm most certain we have the skills and know-how to meet any governmental training and certification."

While Turtle Dove looked at the meeting agenda, Hooded Merganser and Starling shared looks of approval about Starling's cutting remarks.

Turtle Dove suspected a change of energy when he looked up. He noticed the quick diversion of Hooded Merganser's gaze from somewhere else to him and Hooded Merganser's intense look of concentration on his face. "There's been an alignment of forces," Turtle Dove thought to himself. "We'll see. We'll see. It'll show itself at some point." Turtle Dove remembered that he had wanted to share the information he had heard during breakfast with his colleagues right away. Maybe the time was now, he thought, but a sudden awareness made him inhale quickly and deeply. "Don't say anything about it! Don't tell anyone!" he heard an internal voice speak.

Hooded Merganser, because he'd been watching Turtle Dove very closely, inquired, "Were you about to *ask* something, Turtle Dove?"

"Ah-h-h, I was about to say..." Turtle Dove began speaking. Then his throat closed involuntarily, and the inner voice urged again, "Don't say anything about it! Don't tell anyone!"

Turtle Dove smiled nervously, shook his head, and stayed silent. He thought to himself, "So this is what Daddy meant when he'd say, "You gotta move when the Spirit say move." Peacefulness blanketed him as he sat and listened.

Hooded Merganser looked about with an air of satisfaction. Anhinga smiled in pleasure to have witnessed the drama that had unfolded before her. Looking to Great Blue Heron, she commented, "It seems to me that we've talked about everything for today. Right?"

Anhinga moved to the clearing with the others to fly to their homes. "Put on your wings!" she called out. "Put on your wings!"

Barred Owl had seen the secretive exchange of smiles, sneers, and sneakiness throughout the day. And he'd watched Turtle Dove's quizzical response of awareness, knowing that in due season time whatever is done in darkness comes into the light.

"Yes, you'll see, Turtle Dove, you will see," she thought to herself about what Turtle Dove had concluded. "Keep listening and tasting the air. You'll see...."

And there was evening, and there was morning—the fourth day.

CHAPTER FIVE

A PREMONITION ABOUT THE NEXT DAY'S GREAT COUNCIL DISCUSSION HAD made Barred Owl think throughout the night about cackles, hoots, caws, and gurgles. She awoke feeling feisty but, with determination, focused her thoughts on Painted Bunting and Wild Turkey. She'd seen things. Had heard stories. Thinking and blinking, she wished them well.

Great Blue Heron flew in bearing an overnight bag in addition to her typical small suitcase-size purse. The sight caused Great Council members to gather around her quickly.

"He didn't make it through the night, huh?" Rooster clucked. "This novel bird flu is so dangerous! Every year, People name some new disease after us birds. It's People Flu, not Bird Flu! I'm so sorry to hear about your loss."

Great Blue Heron confirmed that her father-in-law had passed. Her husband had been with him when he'd crossed the last river. Her family was traveling now, and she would join them today when she left Angel Oak. The family's Sun Red fa Down Homegoing Service would be at sunset tomorrow.

"They say if you nibble on some Life Everlasting blossoms in the first two hours of feeling bad, you'll make it through this flu-thing okay," Ruddy Duck said. "Make sure you take some with you, now!"

The birds formed a circle around Great Blue Heron and all began trilling "In the Sweet By and By." After expressing their condolences, they pulled away and the meeting began.

"Sister Leader Great Blue Heron," Starling stated as he addressed the group, "please know that I will stand by your side to offer anything you and your family may need during this moment of distress. It is a moment that is not a stranger to any one of us. So, please, please throw out the lifeline, if need be, and I will surely pull you back to shore."

Great Blue Heron nodded in appreciation, and Starling continued. "Stories should be our Thrust. Stories will help Lowcountry birds to know who we are and will help other birds to find commonality with us. Our funeral songs and burial practices, our superstitions and beliefs, everything about us is rooted in a story."

Turtle Dove's wing shot up in the air. Starling turned toward him wearily and said, "Yes, Turtle Dove?"

"That's a great idea, Starling!"

Starling seemed relieved and somewhat caught off guard.

"Thank you," he replied.

Turtle Dove continued, "This could dovetail with what Wood Stork said about Aerial Markers."

"I know. I know."

Others began to join the enthusiasm.

"I remember this story about my mother's mother telling me about callings," Ruddy Duck reminisced. "Sometimes, we'd be a three-generation duck family swimming in a former rice field. Grandma Ruddy would tell me, 'Chile, some bods born wit a callin, ya know.'"

"'A callin? What's that?'" I asked her. 'The sounds we make when we talk to each other?'

"'E a gif, Chile. E de ting de Sperit Bod gii de one E wanfa hab em fa leh ebby body kno how ta git long wid one noda. Ow ta fin jestice. Ow ta stay een de wata an ow fa stay een de air an not die.'

"'I got a 'gif,' Grandma?'

"'Hunnah kno wen hunnah kno, Chile. Sometime, odda peepul kin shem. Me ain see yours yet. E like a tird yeye een de meedle of some bod head.'

"'A third eye, Grandma? What you mean?'

"Dah tird yeye mek some bod see wa odda bods cyan see. Kno wa odda bods cyan kno. An yeddy tings dat odda bods cyan yeh.

"'I wanna gif, Grandma! Please pray to Sperit Bod to give me one.'

"'Now ebby bod wa git a gif dohn use em right. De gif ain fa de bod essef. E fa hep odda bods, fa hep odda life. Som bods gon try fa mek de one wit de gif daark e light. Bot e betta not daark em. E betta leh e light shine fa mek de worl e betta place. Oona yeh me, Chile?'

"'An anodda ting. Dohn need fa git no new nyame wen hunnah git de gif. No need fa tell ebbyboddy bout em or fa tell ebbybody bout de tings hunnah do wen hunnah git de gif. Cause odda bods gon shem. An ef noboddy shem, hunnah jes haffa keep doin de ting Sperit Bod wan em fa do. Widout mek ebby body bow down ta em.'

"'Yes, Grandma Ruddy. If I get a 'gif,' I'm gonna let it shine. And when I see others with a third eye, I'll look to see if they're using their 'gif' to help others or to help themselves. Thanks, Grandma!"

"'A ga pray fa hunnah fa git one. Maybe two. Maybe eben shree!'

"That's what she told me! I remember that story so clearly. I think an Aerial Marker about the importance of Bird Beliefs is something we should plan for."

Great Blue Heron quickly added, "And we've got bird dances and bird calls that are different in our part of the world..."

"Oh, yeah! Here's one," Rooster commented. "There's the mating dance. Don't forget about courtship dances and rituals. Here's what we roosters do. First, we drop a wing and "dance" around the hen in a circle, with the dropped wing held inside. If the rooster's got it going on, the hen will lower her back." Rooster began speaking in a singsong manner, "Now, that's a drop of the wing and a dip in the back. A drop of the wing and a dip in the back." Oh, yes, I'm glad Spirit Bird started *that* dance from the beginning of time. A rooster then mounts the hen, grabbing her by the back of the neck with his beak to steady himself while he does the... the... you know, the Shake Your Tail Feather. Just like Tina Turner sang, 'Bend over and let me see you shake a tail

21

feather. Bend over and let me see you shake a tail feather...' Hah, hah, hah. You know what I mean."

Tufted Titmouse joked, "Stop it, Rooster. You dirty old bird!" "That's just the way, the only way, all Lowcountry Birds keep love and life going on," Rooster cockadoodle-dooed. "It's the good and decent way."

A spring shower of silence fell as the Council members chuckled and gathered their thoughts. It was followed by a rumbling thunderclap.

"No, it's *not* the only way or the only *good and decent way* Lowcountry Birds have been loving and living since the beginning of time," Painted Bunting shot back. "Who are you to make such a judgment call for all Birds of the Air? Now, don't make me pull all these bright feathers off..." The low-range pitch of Painted Bunting's voice began to get higher and softer. "...or I'll tell you what you can do with your 'drop AND your dip.' If *I* want to, I can drop it... (lower voice) ... or I can dip it (higher voice) -- good *and* decent. You hear me? And who you think you rumbling with...?"

Painted Bunting gave Rooster the side-eye, not knowing if he was feigning ignorance or was totally oblivious to the goings-on in his own barnyard.

Great Blue Heron raised one leg and stood stoically looking to the left and to the right. "Order," she said. "Let's bring this meeting back to order. Please."

Turtle Dove raised his wing but immediately began speaking. "If we can, Council members, if we can... can we put our judgments aside and just listen to whatever opinions are voiced? I'm sure Great Blue Heron wants us to make a decision that'll acknowledge everyone -- all Birds of the Lowcountry." He looked to the leader.

"That's right. That is right," Blue Heron said. "We are working on determining the Thrust, the action that will make us -- all of us -- move through the air and continue flying!" Does anyone else have anything to say about the topic? About stories?

Wild Turkey walked to the front, her ample breasts bustling as she moved. "Well, as some of you know, my daughter...well...she struts. She knows other hens who strut, too. And even though she and other hens can't display as brightly as a tom, there are hens and jennies who are attracted to them. These hens do the whole courting ritual. Without a gobbler in sight. One hen drops the wing, and the other lowers the back, she tells me. Some of these hens even gobble. Can you believe that?" She suppressed a quiet guffaw then continued.

"Well, they make it less painful and bloody for the hens who lower their backs, I'm sure. And you know what else? I know toms who want to be with toms. If these hen-hen and tom-tom couples come across abandoned chicks or poults, sometimes they raise them. A new family in the wild! Sometimes, they remain childless couples. But, for the most part, day in and day out, they do what other birds do. They support the ecosystem. They protect our drinking water by preventing erosion. They sing and eat things that destroy crops on farms. What I'm trying to say is this -- we are all Birds of the Lowcountry. And not one of us should be denied to nest in the Tree of Life."

Starling quickly stated, "And any story of merit achieved by any Bird of the Lowcountry should become a part of the Aerial Markers -- if that's the route we choose to take."

Turtle Dove bobbed his head up and down affirmatively, smiling with Starling.

"And don't forget about 'Broke Neck' Nuthatch and others like him," Turtle Dove added.

"That's right," Wood Stork chuckled. "He came out the hole in the tree headfirst and started walking down the tree headfirst, so he didn't see the medium-size twig that snapped and clobbered him down. He wore a neck brace for the rest of his life but that didn't keep him from being a good mate and provider for their brood."

Great Blue Heron looked toward the shade lines on the ground to determine the time of day. Knowing she'd need to leave soon, she announced that after a break she'd select an alternate to lead the Great Council in her absence and that she was considering asking Turtle Dove. Wood Stork and Hooded Merganser each scowled immediately and began thinking of ways to sabotage *that* possibility.

And there was evening, and there was morning—the fifth day.

CHAPTER SIX

BARRED OWL PERCHED ON A LIMB IN ANGEL OAK. THE MORE SHE SAW, the less she spoke. The less she spoke, the more she heard. Great Council members were not like that wise old bird.

Barred Owl was anxious about what would unfold during the day's meeting. Before yesterday's meeting had adjourned and Great Blue Heron had flown away to her family's funeral celebration, a shift in plans had occurred. During the meeting's break, several Great Council members had met with Great Blue Heron individually, proposing who they thought would be a better choice to lead the group during her absence.

Hooded Merganser had petitioned that he was the better choice because he spoke words of wisdom that affirmed birds by helping them to know and appreciate their full potential. He'd argued that Turtle Dove, to the contrary, only pummeled others with questions and criticisms. Hooded Merganser then encouraged a few of his associates to speak on his behalf. They approached Great Blue Heron one by one, but each only trumpeted the beauty of their own bird call.

Wood Stork testified about his committed leadership throughout years of working qualitatively, wing-to-wing, with Bald Eagle. "Why, after all," he touted, "at Bald Eagle's request, I'm the lone sparrow who vetted the selections of the other Council members! During your leave-of-absence, my recognition of strengths, weaknesses, and abilities will prepare you for making good decisions upon your return. And any recommendation of dead leaves, twigs, dry grass, or feathers that I bring to Bald Eagle's attention, most assuredly will be used for the construction of a nest at the highest pinnacle of the highest tree. Now, that's the nest all birders long to see! Don't you agree?

"Besides, strangely enough, Whippoorwill approached me yesterday with an unexpected surprise. She said that she'd awakened *during the daytime*, after nesting, with a belly filled -- almost too filled -- with moths and crickets and that she'd heard Spirit Bird speak to her. She said she'd stayed awake in the sun so long afterward that she felt like a drunken Cedar Waxwing that bounced into windows and glass doors after feasting on overripe berries. She said a majestic voice had commanded her, 'Go tell Wood Stork that he needs you to do whatever he needs you to do.' Now, I know Whippoorwills only sleep during the daytime, and I know eating insects is Whippoorwill's best attribute. But if Spirit Bird sent her to me, then the two of us can oversee getting everything done that needs to be done! Everything! You won't have to ruffle your feathers at all. We'll find a way, cowbird-like, and can just stand stately, poised, and upright -- emanating the values and qualities that represent all Lowcountry birds. With my years of service in the National Order of Fowl History, I can assure that all members will preen about and glorify us."

Starling of Bird Land spoke about his effective and dynamic leadership with the abundant acts of service he and his organizations had performed for Lowcountry birds. "It's what I do," he said in making a closing statement. "We all are songbirds who can sing, and tweet, *an tings lokka dat,* but this is what I do. Every day. Every minute!"

Hovering somewhat differently, Tufted Titmouse preached about her leadership in gifting others with things that benefited them. She confided that Turtle Dove had visited the Matanzas State Forest in St. Augustine, FL, but had not returned with a single fern, berry, or other edible memento for her. And it was she, after all, who had encouraged him to visit the area, she complained. The two of them had been discussing their annoyance in hearing People talk about only having the North Star to guide them along the Underground Railroad. And both she and Turtle Dove could not understand why People only rarely spoke about watching the southern flight of migratory birds during the daytime.

Unlike the others who'd spoken briefly, Tufted Titmouse had continued blistering Great Blue Heron's ears with vain and vapid, self-directed conversation.

"But it was I who informed Turtle Dove that the first route of the Underground Railroad was south – not north – because the enslaved People in the Carolinas escaped to find freedom in Spanish Florida," she'd said. "That's why Turtle Dove flew to St. Augustine in the first place. Now a great leader   would've brought something back to say, 'Thank you!', don't you agree?!?"

Unknown to Hooded Merganser, however, Anhinga had been the last secret visitor that Great Blue Heron had seen. She'd slithered toward her like a silent viper, from the direction opposite the one from which Tufted Titmouse had walked away.

"Oh, Leader Heron, let me bring a matter to your attention, please," Anhinga had said to Great Blue Heron.

"Of course, Anhinga. What can I do for you?"

"I wonder who will receive the coveted Broad-winged Hawk Distinguished Service Award."

"Well, some very interesting ideas have been raised. It'll be up to us to decide who has presented the most significant one. Do you have one to bring to my attention?"

"Oh, no, Great Blue Heron. I don't have any ideas, and I certainly don't need any new awards. My tree condo is filled with them from years of researching and writing and teaching birds to 'Put on Their Wings…'. You know…"

Great Blue Heron smiled and glanced at her overnight bag. "I've got to take to the air soon, Anhinga. Is there anything I can help you with before I go?"

Demonstrating feigned compassion, Anhinga moved closer to Great Blue Heron and touched wingtips.

"I am so sorry to hear about your father-in-law's passing. A few days ago, when we had the election, I chose not to compete because there was sickness in my own family. We didn't know whether our son was going to make it."

"I had no idea! Is he okay?"

"Why, yes, he is. He's on the road to recovery, 'thanks to Spirit Bird,' as you'd hear them say at the Blessed Feather Conventions of the Church of Birds and Unruffled Plumage." She chuckled softly, then continued. "If his condition hadn't improved, we didn't know how we would've financed his care. Things can happen so quickly!"

"Gray skies are gonna clear up, Anhinga. Mark my word." Anhinga lowered her head and inhaled deeply. As if on cue, Great Blue Heron moved to her side and enwrapped Anhinga under her left wing. Anhinga looked up deceitfully, making certain that the faintest physical contact remained intact.

"Thank you so much. Thank you. Now, I want you to know I think you are doing a great job. But since my son's health began to improve, I've been thinking that I should've given you a run for your money the other day."

"I was quite surprised when you didn't and then nominated me!"

"Because you'll be gone... for only a day, am I right? Well, if I could fill this position for only a day of your absence, it would mean so much to me. I'd make sure everything runs smoothly and efficiently until your return. And we can vote on the Distinguished Service Award recipient at that time."

"Well, we've been together on this air current for a very long time, Anhinga. That will be alright with me."

Anhinga smiled demurely. Then to ensure that her talon had pierced and severed any thoughts that would alter Great Blue Heron's decision, she added, "And with all the outstanding work you've done for the Great Council so far, you want to make sure no other little birdie steps in with the unmitigated gaul and temerity to make *their* actions *stand out* more! Don't you agree?"

The two leaders soon departed.

Barred Owl listened and thought. "That was yesterday. Today is today. Out of one, many. Out of many, one bird is to be knocked down and licked clean. 'Live with vultures, become a vulture; live with crows, become a crow.'"

Arriving early, Anhinga greeted each Council member cordially with outstretched wings. Great Blue Heron had announced Anhinga as her temporary replacement before she'd departed.

"I give you my support in any idea you may present today," he told Turtle Dove with a smile of reassurance.

To Hooded Merganser, he implored, "The idea you spoke about when you were nominated has merit. If you propose it as an idea for Thrust, it may need a little tweaking but I'll help guide you along the way, if necessary. I've learned lots of things along those lines as Founder and CEO of Wishbone Intel."

Happy not to be under Turtle Dove's leadership for the day, Hooded Merganser was hopeful that Turtle Dove wouldn't bring another idea to the table today. If he did, Hooded Merganser was prepared to use the right words to affirm to Turtle Dove how he regarded him: as an instigator and a critic.

"I'm happy to stand before you today, on behalf of our Leader who has assembled with her family today. This is our last day to discuss ideas about what will be our Thrust or action that will make us move through the air and continue flying! So far, we've heard from Tufted Titmouse, Wood Stork, and Starling. Does anyone else have anything to be considered?"

All eyes turned to Turtle Dove. Only a few had interacted with him throughout the morning, feeling anxious and perplexed about the apparent slight he'd experienced following the break during yester-day's meeting. He smiled comfortably and gestured that he had nothing to comment. With growing confidence, Hooded Merganser slowly raised his wing.

"Hooded Merganser, what would you like to propose?" Anhinga asked.

"Well, I'm sure you all remember my discussion the day we first came together," he began. He looked at Cedar Waxwing, who swiftly turned her head in the opposite direction and crossed her wings, refusing to engage with him throughout his presentation.

"I apologize if I offended anyone that day." He waited momentarily to see if he'd regained Cedar Waxwing's attention but continued slowly without it. "I still believe the importance of a name is very important…"

Cedar Waxwing hmf-ed heavily and rolled her eyes.

"…but I'm one with everyone else in maintaining the name of the law -- as it stands now -- as the Audubon Rookery."

A collective sigh of relief spread below the tree limbs.

"Our Thrust should be in knowing and understanding those birds who are like us. Some pigeons and gulls followed the slave ships from Africa all the way to the Lowcountry. Some birds in Jamaica, the West Indies, and Haiti tell their children the same "Buh Crow" stories. And my friends in Brazil and some West African countries say the People there talk about seeing and feeling a Hag, whatever that is, on their chests some nights -- just like the People here talk about."

Anhinga spoke when Hooded Merganser paused. "And don't forget, whenever we communicate with other birds in this country, they are often confused about where we're from and ask if we are from one of the countries that you just mentioned."

"Yes, our songs, our calls, our rituals with birds of these countries are all connected," Hooded Merganser said. He flinched as he saw Turtle Dove's wing rising out of the corner of his eye. With a sullen look on his face, he turned to face him.

"Do you think that inflections of pitch in bird shrieks in these other countries could have the same meanings as ours or that some of the burial practices could be similar?" Turtle Dove asked.

Hooded Merganser froze like a deer caught in a car driver's head-lights. "Maybe. I don't know. Is that important?" he responded when able. He tried to think of questions or comments he could hurl out to deflect Turtle Dove's concentration, to impale him on a skewer in preparation for a spitroast. Turtle Dove's questions irritated him, and his comments always seemed overly critical. They made his breathing quicken and his face flush.

"Yeah, I see where you travelin, Turtle Dove," Cedar Waxwing commented. "Sometimes I shriek high at the end to ask a question, or I shriek low at the end to make a statement. Like, 'Goin to the bird feeda?' or 'Goin to the bird feeda!' Same shriek, different meaning. The Jamaican Spindalis does the same thing."

Before Ruddy Duck added to the conversation, Hooded Merganser had begun to relax.

"We'll need to explore if Brazilian birds do the same things at funerals like we do," Ruddy Duck said with fascination. "Great Blue Heron most likely will tell us when he returns that the grandbaby birds were passed three times over the Granddaddy Bird lying on the ground. And that the weeping relatives scattered quickly to eat some Carolina Gold rice and taste some Scuppernong grape wine before the scavenger birds and animals came to do what they do. I bet Brazilian birds eat grains of funeral rice. Oh, this topic is good. This is good!"

"Well, it seems we now have four proposals," Anhinga concluded. "I'd like the four presenters to take some time to think about their ideas. In a little while, I'd like them to come to the front to answer any questions we may have. That way, when Great Blue Heron returns tomorrow, we'll be ready to vote on the one proposal that we think is best."

Gaining consensus, Anhinga continued. "Before we take a break for the presenters to review their proposals, let's talk about the business idea I pitched to some of you yesterday.

"What idea was that?" Turtle Dove asked. "It must've been discussed before I arrived."

"I've received a partnership request to promote a project that'll produce foods for Lowcountry Birds," Anhinga stated.

As the words "partnership," "promote," and "produce" left Anhinga's lips, Turtle Dove's head froze. His throat constricted. And with eyes wide-opened, he stared blankly in Anhinga's direction.

"He's bent on selling us on a business that's not by Lowcountry birds," Seagull snipped. "One that'll produce some kind of product for Lowcountry birds. And that'll somehow benefit Lowcountry birds only by making other birds want to be like us!"

"What's...the name...of...this...business?" Turtle Dove struggled to ask. In his mind, he again heard the still, silent voice commanding, "Don't say anything about it! Don't tell anyone!" And then, his own voice vanished like the last patch of fog on a full sunshiny morning. His wingtips lifted to lightly touch his throat.

Turtle Dove's strange behavior signaled that he was about to stymie the discussion, Anhinga thought. So, she moved in front of Seagull, although it was not Seagull who had not asked the last question.

"It's the Bobolink Bird Feed, LLC," Anhinga announced proudly but softly.

Turtle Dove's eyes rolled around in their sockets and his gaze slowly followed Anhinga's movements.

"They'd like to use the name *Audubon Rookery* on their packaging," Anhinga continued. "And they've pledged to use a picture of Lowcountry Birds only, changing seasonally with a group picture of various bird types. It'll provide fabulous marketing for our Rookery, and they'll make a sizable donation to any project that we'd like."

All birds looked at each other incredulously.

"Well, we certainly can't do anything about this until Great Blue Heron hears about it!" Ruddy Duck said. Great Council members nodded in agreement.

"And Bald Eagle should know about this, too," said Wood Stork.

Tufted Titmouse inquired, "Has any paperwork been submitted? Hopefully, no one has signed off on anything."

"Fishy," Seagull grunted. "Something smells fishy!"

"What do you mean?" Anhinga asked.

"What I mean," Seagull purred, "is what's in this for you, Anhinga? Hmmm?"

Scurrying to change the subject, Anhinga moved on to another topic. "Well, that's enough about that for now," he concluded. "Will the presenters of the four proposals please come forward when I call your name. Idea One is about Healthy Eating by Tufted Titmouse. Idea Two is about Aerial Markers by Wood Stork. Idea Three is about Stories by Starling. And, last, Idea Four is about Audubon Diaspora by Hooded Merganser. These ideas are exemplary! Please ask any questions about them to gain clarity for tomorrow's vote."

Questions were asked. Answers were given. And changes were

made. With the exception, that is, of one that Turtle Dove had hoped to express. But he had no voice.

"So have we completed this exercise with satisfaction?" Anhinga asked. "If all hearts are at peace, we'll present four ideas to Great Blue Heron tomorrow."

Turtle Dove timidly raised his wing. Anhinga nodded for him to speak, but Turtle Dove could only grunt and mutter.

"Yes, Turtle Dove?" Anhinga asked. "What is it?"

Turtle Dove touched his wingtips together, resting them as one unit to his throat and blinked his eyes. Anhinga thought he was making an unnecessary scene. Turtle Dove had wanted to suggest that only one proposal should be made in the morning. That the four separate proposals were unnecessary because some of the ideas that had been presented could fit under three newly named headings. That a combination of all three were needed to achieve Thrust.

Pointing his right wing again and again at Anhinga to communicate that only one proposal would be needed made Anhinga think she was being confronted, perhaps about the partnership proposal.

"So, you think I've done something wrong?" Anhinga asked, beginning to pace back and forth.

Turtle Dove shook his head back and forth repeatedly to signify that Anhinga's conclusion was incorrect. Anhinga miscalculated the movement to mean that Turtle Dove believed that nothing she'd said was true, that she'd been lying by commission.

Pausing and attempting a new communication tactic, Turtle Dove continued shaking his head while looking at his left wing and pointing it at Anhinga in intervals of four. He would then turn his head to look at his right wing while pointing it at Anhinga in intervals of three. "Four proposals don't state what's best for us," he'd hoped Anhinga would understand. "Three proposals do."

Anhinga thought Turtle Dove was losing his mind.

"You're as cracky as a Loon!" Anhinga sniped.

Hoping to somehow break through with understanding, Turtle Dove rubbed his temples with his wingtips and then changed movements. He clasped his wings together and lifted them up, meaning "only one proposal was needed" and then opened them to his sides and flapped up and down, meaning "the one proposal would help them to fly."

Anhinga was done! Losing any semblance of dignity, she yelled, "Stop it!"

Turtle Dove lowered his wings and stared oddly at Anhinga. All members of the Great Council did, too.

"Aw, look," Anhinga snarled. "Turtle Dove done drooped his wings. What makes you think I've done anything wrong? All your questions and all your comments. As though you think you're the smartest bird up in here. What's the matter? Cat's got your tongue. No one has done anything to you. Sometimes, when you spend all your time helping others, sometimes you've got to realize that you'd better help yourself... I can tell you don't know that yet. Right?"

When her ranting stopped, Anhinga realized that others had been watching her in bewilderment. She lifted her head high and, before walking to the outskirts of the tree limbs, said, "'Put on your wings. When we get to heaven, gonna put on our wings.' This meeting is adjourned!"

And there was evening, and there was morning—the sixth day.

CHAPTER SEVEN

BARRED OWL HAD WATCHED THE 25 GREAT COUNCIL MEMBERS COME AND go for the past six days. Her daily early morning mantra had been "A bird never flew on one wing!" The Great Council's Mission had been to select one proposal for Thrust. One leader had been elected to corral the thoughts of many. Conundrums pelted her thoughts. Would the Audubon Rookery successfully achieve liftoff? How many Great Council members had participated only to jockey for a higher perch of public perception? To manifest selfishness? To try to impress others? How many had allowed only a few others to bear the burden of being buffeted by gale winds of opposition and distrust and who now felt as though they'd been in the storm so long.

She hummed a tune as the Council members arrived with their mates and partners,

"I got a new home over in Glory
And it's mine, mine, mine.
I got a new home over in Glory
And it's mine, mine, mine."

Early the next morning, Hooded Merganser and Turtle Dove eyed each other walking about on the opposite ends of Angel Oak. They'd arrived separately, each with plans to ground himself before the day's event began. The fervor of Barred Owl's song inspired the two birds to move toward each other.

"We've got to talk," Hooded Merganser said politely. "Would that be okay?"

"Any time is the right time...to come together...to heal...to live and let live," Turtle Dove answered. "Are any of those what you have in mind?"

"With respect, I think we got off on the wrong webbed foot," Hooded Merganser said. "There are some things you do that I find offensive. And maybe there are things I do that you don't like." They nodded in agreement. "I just got to say, when you ask those million-and-one questions during our meetings, I feel set-up as though I'm a duck decoy and you're trying to take me out!"

Turtle Dove twisted his head in amazement. "Some birds sing or cluck or caw to communicate a thought," he stated. "Now, others make sounds--pretty sounds, interesting sounds--in order to think about whatever it is they may want to communicate. The flight pattern or flight span of their thoughts has not yet been determined, so they call out these disconnected sounds until they are certain of the fuller message of their communication journey."

He looked to make certain that Hooded Merganser was understanding him.

"That's why I ask questions, Hooded Merganser. To help some to see the thought-puzzle-pieces that they may be trying to put together. They may speak it, but I can see it. At other times, when some birds twitter, hoot, or chirp, they may think that what they're messaging means the same thing to whatever bird is listening. But it doesn't always. Blue Jay's 'Twitter, twitter' may mean 'Come here, show me some love!' while Buzzard's 'Twitter, twitter' could mean, 'Step closer and I'll pick your bones clean!' So, I ask questions."

Hooded Merganser placed his wingtip over his beak, requesting Turtle Dove to pause. "I always thought you were being critical,"

Merganser shrieked. "That you were acting like you thought you were better than anyone else."

"That's not it," Turtle Dove cooed. "Others may see themselves speaking one thing, but I hear the confusion their messaging may be causing. So, I may try to use different sounds that I think convey the same meaning. And then I ask if the sounds I suggested mean the same thing to them as what the other bird had spoken. Usually, they find they've been saying the same thing but with different sounds that carry different meanings for each of them."

"That's deep, my Bird!" Hooded Merganser said. "That's deep! But, here's another thing. That is, if you don't mind my asking?"

"Well, I won't know until I hear it."

Hooded Merganser stared at Turtle Dove's beak for a few minutes. "Okay, okay... I was waiting to see if you saw my question before I spoke it."

Turtle Dove's eyes and smile danced on his face. "No, not this time...at least, not yet..."

"Well, sometimes, when you're asking a question or making a statement, if another bird interrupts you...," Hooded Merganser began.

"'...why do I begin to act agitated and speak differently?' Is that what you were going to ask?" Turtle Dove concluded.

"Well, grea-ea-ea-ea-t day!" Hooded Merganser howled. "You saw it! Before I said it!"

Turtle Dove shrugged his shoulders, then looked briefly to the east. "That started during my childhood," he turr-ed. "Mama told me my behavior is like my Uncle Aaron's. He died before I was born, so I never knew him. I don't know if what she said is true or not. I think my behavior is because I was the ninth and last chick in the brood. Well, he was born into a large family, too. There were five of them, but there were four more of us!

"My older siblings must have had stronger lungs than I did, I guess. Cause although Turtle Dove calls are only 'turr-turr' and 'perch-oo' and 'coo,' when they all started clamoring, I could never think straight! I'd stumble with a 'tur-perch' or an 'oo-coo.' Whoever heard of such? And each one of them would one-amp-up the other until the ruckus would send my thoughts into a tailspin. When that happens, the words I want to use begin to spin around in my head, zigging here and zagging there.

"I slow down my speech. So that I can snatch the words up. In time to attach them to the next word that's floating by in my mind. And in time so that all my connected words make sense."

"Whew, Bird, that's a lot!" said Hooded Merganser.

"And if I speak louder during those slow-speaking times, it's not because I'm yelling at anyone. It's an increased volume-level of frustration with myself -- not with anyone else -- because someone's interruption. Or look of confusion. Or expression that maybe I'm some kind of dodo bird...All those things keep the words spinning around behind my eyes. And I'm trying, my best, to slow them down. So that the conversation can continue. Understood?"

"That's dope, Turtle Dove! That's dope. You know, what you said about your childhood, makes me know that sometimes I need to go back and talk to my Inner Two-Month-Old Hooded Merganser."

"And what would you tell him?" Turtle Dove asked.

"Well, I'd say, 'Hoody-who, when Daddy asks, 'Now, why didn't you dive down deeper in the pond before eating that grasshopper on the surface?', he's not saying you're a dummy. He just wants you to realize that your Merganser eyes are so gangsta, they can see underwater and that you don't need to fill up on an insect-appetizer when the crustaceans below will keep me energized for a much longer time.

"And, 'Hood Boi, when Daddy says, 'What you see over there, Son?', and all you see is a big rock, it's not a test to confirm that he thinks you're cock-eyed or something or that there's something else there that you need to see. No, he just wants you to know that if you're swimming and get tired, that rock is a place that you can swim to, then rest and meditate. Or that if something is chasing you, there's a spot you can hide behind until danger passes.

"I'd tell my Little Me, 'Yo Daddy loves you! And when you have a little Merganser child, you better love him or her. With that same kinda love. That deep kinda love that hurts even when you don't want it to hurt. And you better teach them what they need to know so they can fly right."

Just as they finished their dayclean conversation, the other Great

Council members arrived with their guests. Hooded Merganser's and Turtle Dove's mates flew in a few minutes after each other and from the opposite direction of Mr. and Mrs. Great Blue Heron. The agitation in the air was as thick as kudzu. Leaving their guests behind, Seagull and Starling hurried to convene privately with their Leader.

"Oh, it ain pretty!" Starling said.

"If we lyin, we flyin," Seagull added. "And right now, as you see for yourself, our feet. are on. the. ground!"

"Well, I'll be!" Great Blue Heron said in unbelief after listening to them. "Is this so?" She paused and then cautioned, "If things are as you say they are, all we can do is wait. A new net won't catch an old bird. And no matter how high a bird flies, it has to come down for water."

In addition to invited guests, the day, with its expected pageantry, brought together community wildlife members, media representatives, People, Lowcountry birds who were Great Council wannabes disgruntled about not having been selected, and plain old gawkers looking for something to talk about.

Great Blue Heron opened the meeting with expressions of grati- tude to many. To Spirit Bird for bringing us to this moment. To Bald Eagle for the vision of the new law. To Ancestral and Elder Lowcountry birds and Lowcountry birds far and near for being who we have been and are. And last but not least, to Great Council members for their wisdom, dedication, and labor of love over the past six days.

Council member and Mr. Anhinga had arrived after the meeting began, so Great Blue Heron had not had an opportunity to speak with her beforehand. She motioned for Anhinga to come to the front to call out the proposals and the visionaries for Thrust, the activity by which the Audubon Rookery would work to help Lowcountry birds to attain and to continue flying at new altitudes. She informed all that afterward a vote would be taken by Great Council members to identify the most effective proposal and that the visionary would receive a distinguished service award.

"Click, click! Good day, everyone! Click, click!" Anhinga sounded with aplomb. "I'm pleased to inform you of the four proposal ideas that have been generated. Great Blue Heron, would you like the visionaries to stand when their names are called?"

As Great Blue Heron nodded to Anhinga, she noticed Turtle Dove's wing rising in the audience. Anhinga's face soured, and she looked at her husband with consternation.

"Yes, Turtle Dove?" Great Blue Heron asked.

"Before we vote, I'd like to..."

Mr. Anhinga opened and then loudly snapped his beak closed. Then his eyes led his head to follow an imaginary insect, and he bumped into other birds for a few moments before making an exaggerated faux catch in his mouth and a flourishing swallow down his elongated throat. The commotion had caused its predetermined distraction. He twisted his neck in imagined pleasure and sighed with gustatory satisfaction. Then, he blinked at his wife before settling down.

Great Blue Heron looked again to Turtle Dove to continue.

"If I may, before we take a vote, I'd like to..."

Anhinga began to cough. A soft cough. Then a louder cough. Then a cacophony of bogus coughing! Regaining suspect composure, she glowered at Turtle Dove, as though daring him to continue any attempt to communicate.

"I'd like to hear what Turtle Dove has to s...," Hooded Merganser stated. But Anhinga deflected as though she hadn't heard him and began announcing the names of the proposals.

"Proposal One by Council Member Tufted Titmouse promotes programs about Healthy Eating and Lifestyles."

Great Council members, all a bit flummoxed about the goings-on, began to rise as their names were called and to applaud each person who stood.

"Proposal Two by Council Member Wood Stork would make Aerial Markers available to provide geographical directions and enforcement of travel regulations for all who visit our Audubon Rookery." More applause. "Now, the proposal calls for 'Aerial Markers,' but I'm taking the liberty to rephrase these as 'Air Markers' because, well, I'm not sure every Lowcountry bird would readily understand what 'aerial' means. You know about the lack of education among some of us..."

Anhinga began to snicker. But looking up and seeing glares of disapproval, she attempted to correct herself. "'Air markers'... 'Air markers' is just easier to say," she stated.

She continued, "Proposal Three by Council Member Starling encourages implementation of stories that declare the unique idiosyncrasies and cultural peculiarities of Lowcountry birds."

Starling, seeing movement on the horizon, moved quickly to the outskirts of Angel Oak as applause began. Seagull exited with him.

"And last," Anhinga concluded with grandiosity, "is Proposal Four by Council Member Hooded Merganser. "Its programs would showcase the Audubon Diaspora of Lowcountry birds and their cultural connections with birds whose ancestral lineage began in West Africa."

Thunderous applause for the combined proposals rose and fell like Lowcountry high and low tides.

Like an arrow, Turtle Dove's wing again shot to the air.

"Turtle Dove...," Anhinga said drily to him and then turned away to address the audience. "Just yesterday Turtle Dove had drooped his wings and could not find any words within him." Anhinga pivoted to look at Turtle Dove shamefully. "Has your voice returned today, Turtle Dove?" She paused, then taking aim like a huntsman shooting skeet, she fired. "Well, put on your wings. When we get to heaven, gonna put on our..."

Starling and Seagull, like guided missiles, flew to the front of the group. "She should not be before this body!" Starling shouted. "Her actions are corrupt, and her alliances are despicable. She does not have the best interests of Audubon Rookery at heart!"

Seeing sudden movement in the audience, Seagull called out, "Oh, no, stop right there!" Anhinga had swiftly joined her husband in an aisle, as they were plotting a quick retreat. "Stay here with the rest of us Audubon Rookery Great Council members, Anhinga. We've got things to talk about..."

Turning to Great Blue Heron, Seagull said quietly, "I'd like to suggest that you call an executive session soon to discuss an urgent matter. Starling has got birdseed receipts!"

Perturbed to be put on blast, Anhinga responded menacingly with croaks and glares. "So, who do you think you are, Starling? Acting so high and mighty? As though you're an Egyptian Nightjar. Seagull squeals about your luminescence, but even the Star of Bethlehem pointed the way to something greater than itself.

"Deceit and corruption are crouching at your nest and they desire to have you! Are you Starling now? Or Starling...of Bird Land? Hmmmm? And just what is Bird Land?!?

"You're hiding dirt that's just camouflaged as sand. With all your fowl rituals and fanfare -- the preening, the dancing, the singing, the displaying -- that require every bird to bow before you. Time will tell.... Wait and see. Time will tell...!

Struggling to regain control, Great Blue Heron looked over the puzzled bird faces.

"Order! Let's have order!" she said. "Turtle Dove, there seems to be something you've been trying to say." Turtle Dove nodded, and Great Blue Heron spoke to all. "Well then, we are going to hear from Turtle Dove and, after that, I'll accept a motion to move into executive session."

"I move right now that we listen to Council member Turtle Dove and then move into the Executive Session," Starling stated.

"And I so-o-o-o second that!" Ruddy Duck followed up.

Turtle Dove smiled at his wife across the aisle way and moved to the front.

"We Great Council members were asked to consider ideas that would move the Audubon Rookery forward. You've just heard four excellent proposals, for which we've been asked to select the one that we believe is the most important. Well, Great Blue Heron and fellow Council members, I think they are all too important to shoot down any one of them.

"Let's just mix up the ingredients of each proposal and season it with a little bit of that and a dash of that, which all of us conversed about. Next, we'll categorize them, and then let's see how this new bird seed tastes. Okay?"

Council members were enthusiastic to continue.

"Well, Tufted Titmouse's idea about healthy eating and Bobolink's thoughts about the importance of trees for habitats and food sources all involve Education. Starling's idea about our stories seemed to have made a great impact on all of us. We talked about callings and beliefs and burial practices and bird calls…"

Council members and guests responded with "Mm-hmms" and wing flaps.

"Well, all these things require Documentation and Preservation. And one way to preserve these stories would be to include them on the Aerial Markers -- not Air Markers, that is -- that Wood Stork proposed.

"And the last thing to bring to your attention is this. Wood Stork also spoke about the need for birds, especially Lowcountry birds, to enforce travel regulations that'll need to be determined. Now, we'll need all types of Lowcountry birds -- and we've got to be inclusive about weight and size and gender and sexual orientation -- to get this work done. And this would involve Economic Development.

"Is this new bird seed tasting good to ya yet?" With no negative response from the audience, Turtle Dove high-tailed his comments on to a conclusion. "This is what we all talked about. I think one proposal that promotes Education, Documentation and Preservation, and Economic Development would give us the Thrust that we need."

Hooded Merganser began a slow wingtip-clap roll. The momentum built, and others joined in, wingtip-clapping faster and faster, louder and louder.

"T.D., that's what I'm talkin bout," Hooded Merganser whooped. "This '3-in-1' that you laid out….Bird, it will please the Elder SkyHawks. It will give every Lowcountry bird the recognition we so rightly deserve. And it will make hatchlings and chicks want to go back to the old landmarks but in ways that are honorable but meaningful to them! Oo-oo-oo-oo-oo-oo!"

Seeking to sow good seeds, Anhinga said with excitement, "Put on your wings….!"

Her words propelled an inflection point and unleashed the whirlwind.

"Put.on.My.Wings, Anhinga?" Turtle Dove began. As their eyes locked gazes, Turtle Dove consciously captured and connected each word swirling behind his eyes, adorned them in vituperation, and released them to maim, rupture, or annihilate. "You.SNAKE BIRD…You betta.put.on.YOURS!   And.when.you.do…where.will.YOU.fly? To

Heaven? No-o-o-o-o-o. To help others? I.don't.think.so! Seems like your wings only deliver you to places where you can damn others and.uplift.who? You.Yourself.And.Yours."

Trying to calm the storm, Great Blue Heron interrupted. "Turtle Dove, I think you are being a bit terse," she said quietly.

Turtle Dove's gaze turned to listen respectfully, but returned, at the conclusion of Great Blue Heron's remark, set upon Anhinga like a guided missile.

"What.YOU.do. What.YOU'VE.done. That's all you seem to talk about   lately....Did.YOU.bring.any.of.those.'*accomplishments*'.with you.when.you cracked your way.out of your eggshell? And the ravens won't see any of them...Any.of. them...neither.when they.fight each other.to clean up.what's.left of.your pompous carcass.

"And.what.did.you.think.keeping ME quiet.would do? Hanh? I didn't wish any harm on you! On any.body! I.just.do.what Spirit Bird.tells ME to do."

Slowly, Turtle Dove averted his intense attentiveness away from Anhinga's deflated facial expression. Taking deep breaths to regain his composure, his chest expanded and released, expanded and released.

Mrs. Turtle Dove walked over to her mate. She nestled her beak to his, gently clasped her right wing around him, and said, "Coo, turr- turr. Coo. Coo-coo."

Great Blue Heron announced that the Great Council would convene an Executive Session. Council members bunched themselves in small groups, trying to make small talk. As media reps, community members, and guests exited to a nearby loblolly pine field, Sandpiper skittered next to Ruddy Duck.

"Well! Mmm, I know, I really haven't had much to say during these meetings," Sandpiper said. "Whenever I had an idea, I'd tell myself, 'Now who would want to hear what Sandpiper has to say?'" She chuckled nervously at her words of self-deprecation. "But it's been an experience I would never have imagined I would've been asked to participate in. Or to witness. Like all that just went on.... And I really, I mean REALLY liked the story you shared about your Grandma Ruddy. It meant so much to me!"

Great Blue Heron signaled to them and others that it was time for

Great Council members to gather. Smiling brightly as she waddled, Ruddy Duck quacked, "Thank you, Sandpiper. It's not too late to participate." She paused to feign making hobbling movements with her feet and knees to demonstrate her words. "Seems like this executive session is going to get real.... r-o-c-k-y! You know what I mean?"

"Well," Sandpiper interrupted in a whispered voice, "I've overheard some things said about Anhinga in a treetop or two."

"Like what?" Ruddy asked.

"Like how she has not always treated every bird in a respectable manner or not always flown in a direct flight from here to there when conducting birdy business. You know, been treating some fowls foul in order to get what was best for herself. Now, she never did anything untoward to me, and I never thought she would do anything that could jeopardize the reputation of this Council, so I just shrugged it off as hearsay...cause, who can deny it? ... she knows a lot of things and she knows a lot of chickadees."

"Well, well, well," Ruddy Duck answered. "What I know is this: if you see or hear of some bird pooping on another bird and you don't say or do anything about it, soon and very soon, when you least expect it -- S-P-L-A-T-T! -- that same bird will surely poop right on you! Right now, though, at this executive session, is your time to help set the record straight. It's your duty and it takes a "gif" of courage to do it.

"And I've got to say, Sandpiper, all of us Lowcountry birds got a 'gif' -- like Grandma Ruddy told me about. But, Gur-r-l-l-l, are you feeling it yet? I've never experienced anything like it."

"What are you talking about, Ruddy Duck?"

"Turtle Dove turned our V-flight pattern around so-o-o-o fast, we'll be dealing with whiplash for days. No, for years! Now, fa true! For him to do that took having not just one gift. But two. Or three.

"You know, down through the years, we just may see that a lot of Lowcountry birds in this Great Council had some serious self-propelling plans."

"Amen to that!" Sandpiper sounded with a wheet-wheet-wheet.

Ruddy Duck responded with wisdom learned from the elders.

"Bot ebry bod wa got wings, kin only fly high as e wings take em. No matta wa e say or do. An dem wa bon fa fly high, ga fly high --

eben wen oddas tell em say, 'Oona cyan do dat.' bot day see em do dat wit e ownt two yeye!

"Sandpiper, dat de trute ebby bod haffa go tweet."

By the end of the seventh day, the Audubon Rookery had achieved Thrust by pledging to follow a three-tiered implementation plan, for which all Great Council members had worked. Each received a Broad-winged Hawk Distinguished Service Award, though Wood Stork felt disillusioned that it had not been given solely to him.

For committing unlawful organizational representation and receipt of payments, Anhinga had been removed from the Great Council and her record of participation had been expunged. Copies of signed checks to Anhinga from Bobolink Bird Feed, LLC and documents that revealed plans to manufacture bird seed that included imported plastic particles from China had been uncovered by the Wade in the Water Webbers and the Birds-of-paradise Playas and were submitted by Starling of Bird Land during the executive session.

Bald Eagle, decisive in timing and commitment, declared in a press statement read by Great Blue Heron, "I want the greatness of the Audubon Rookery to be known throughout this country! Therefore, the rookery's first project of liftoff should be slated from right here -- the majestic limbs of Angel Oak because of its historical significance to Lowcountry birds."

And on a day-to-day basis afterward, Barred Owl has watched the unfolding of a vision -- below the limbs of Angel Oak and beyond -- among poults and parents, mating birds and Elder SkyHawks, comeyah birds, beenyah birds, preening peacocks, and nondescript birds from throughout the world: an environment that celebrates the legacy and continuing contributions of Lowcountry birds to our American Audubon heritage.

"Sing hallelu!" Barred Owl hooted.

And the responding words of the Lowcountry spiritual resounded throughout the Audubon Rookery. "Sing hallelu! Sing hallelu, down in the valley. Sing hallelu!"

THANK YOU

Thank you for reading book 2 in the Gullah Literature Series

www.rondaise.com

If you loved *Turtle Dove Done Drooped His Wings I would love a review. A review helps authors and are very much appreciated.*

Here is your link:
Turtle Dove Done Drooped His Wings

https://amazon.com/B09ZTGDYQ2

ABOUT RON DAISE

Ron Daise, a son of St. Helena Island, SC, and a resident of Georgetown, SC, has authored several books and served as a cultural interpreter for decades. He, his wife Natalie, and their children starred in Nick Jr. TV's *"Gullah Gullah Island."* He also is a former chairman of the federal Gullah Geechee Cultural Heritage Corridor Commission and is vice president for Creative Education at Brookgreen Gardens, Murrells Inlet, SC.

Thank You for Reading and please come visit me on Social Media.

www.rondaise.com
https://instagram.com/gullahron
https://facebook.com/rondaise

Other Books by Ron Daise

Books

- McKenzie Beach Memories, Ford, Johnny L. and Daise, Ron, (CLASS Publishing, 2020)
- Gullah Branches, West African Roots (Sandlapper Publishing, 2006)
- Little Muddy Waters, A Gullah Folk Tale (G.O.G. Enterprises, 1999)
- De Gullah Storybook (fa laarn fa count from 1-10) (G.O.G. Enterprises, 2000)
- Reminiscences of Sea Island Heritage, Legacy of Freedmen on St. Helena Island, Sandlapper Publishing, 1986)

Selected Writings

- "Ancient Voices Beckoning, Pleading" in State of the Heart: SC Writers on the Places They Love (USC Press, 2016)

Recordings

- A Hushed Thrill: Brookgreen Gardens, CD of eight songs about Brookgreen Gardens written by Ron Daise in collaboration with music students and staff of Coastal Carolina University (Athenaeum Press, 2016)
- Gullah Tings fa Tink Bout, CD of songs, poetry and readings from "Gullah Branches, West African Roots" (Ron and Natalie Daise, 2014)

42056342R00037